Real Street Music

Chasing Action

Brayden,

Chase your dreams!!!

Quentin Holmes

This book is printed on acid-free paper.

This book is a work of fiction. Places, events, and situations in this book are purely fictional and any resemblance to actual persons, living or dead, is coincidental.

Printed in the United States of America

CONTENTS

CHAPTER ONE 1

CHAPTER TWO 11

CHAPTER THREE 17

CHAPTER FOUR.. 31

CHAPTER FIVE 37

CHAPTER SIX.. 45

CHAPTER SEVEN 51

CHAPTER EIGHT 61

CHAPTER NINE.. 67

CHAPTER TEN... 73

CHAPTER ELEVEN... 79

CHAPTER TWELVE 89

EPILOGUE.. 101

CHAPTER ONE

Q WOBBLED UNCERTAINLY on the bike, using his feet to steady himself. He looked at his dad. "I don't think I can do this."

"You can do it," his father reassured him.

Q looked at the expanse of concrete sidewalk ahead of him. *That's going to hurt if I fall*, he thought to himself.

"Don't be afraid, I'll catch you if you fall," his father said, as if reading his thoughts.

Q regarded him skeptically. "You're going to run alongside me the whole way?"

His dad nodded and smiled. "The whole way. I'll always be there to catch you. Promise."

Q swallowed hard and put a foot on the pedal and pushed down. Then another. Then another. He wobbled a bit but caught his balance, and suddenly the scenery of his Brooklyn, New York neighborhood started whipping past him at an alarming rate. There was a fruit stand! And the coffee shop! And the bakery!

"That's it, Q! That's it!" he heard his father call after him.

He was doing it! He was riding a bike! The feeling was powerful, as if he was gliding through the air!

"Dad! I'm doing it!" Q sang into the air. "You don't need me!" he heard his father say.

"Wait, Dad!" Q slowed to a stop and turned the bike around. "Dad? DAD?!"

His father was gone.

Q bolted awake. Where was he? His bed was on the wrong side of the room, and instead of the smell of Mrs. Bendetto's famous marinara sauce wafting through the open window, it smelled salty. Like the ocean.

That's when it hit him. He wasn't home.

Q scrounged up a pair of shorts and a t-shirt from his duffel bag. He realized he had to stop thinking that way. He was home. At his new home, anyway. While the events of the last couple of weeks seemed like a dream, they weren't. They were real. And there wasn't a thing he could do about it.

His father was dead.

He wondered how many mornings he'd wake up, confused, only to relive the nightmare. There was the phone call from the police about his father's car accident; Then sitting in the funeral home trying to be strong for his baby sisters, Akara and Amaria. The cross-country trip in the back of his grandparents' minivan while he watched cornfield after cornfield put even more distance between his old life in Brooklyn and his new one in Long Beach, California. Unpacking in the spare bedroom at his grandparents' house, the bedroom was no longer the spare bedroom but *his* bedroom; his grandparents, whom he loved but didn't really know except for the occasional summer vacation and phone calls on his birthday, called him Quincy when they knew that he liked to be called Q.

It was a nickname that his mother invented when he complained that the name Quincy had "too many loops" when he was learning to write in cursive. He thought it sounded kind of cool and it stuck. His sisters, his friends, even his teachers at school called him Q. When his mother died after a long battle with breast cancer when he was in second grade, he thought about going back to the name Quincy, since the nickname Q was a reminder of his mother who was no longer there.

But his dad convinced him that this was a good thing. *She'll always be in our hearts*, he had said, *but every time I call you Q, it's like she's back here, sitting in the room with us.*

Now his father was gone, too. Q went to the window and shut it. Without the ocean breeze, the room grew stuffy and hot with the mid-June heat. It seemed only right. Why should he be here, all comfortable in his bedroom like he was on vacation and having a good time when his father was gone?

He grabbed the pillow off his bed and threw it at the wall, knocking the tacks out of the skateboard poster that he had put up on the wall trying to make the room seem more like home. The poster slid off the wall and Q grabbed it, tearing it to shreds. This place shouldn't be like home. It wasn't home! Brooklyn was home! His dad was home! It was unfair!

"Q? Everything okay up there?" he heard his Grandma Clara call out. "Why don't you come downstairs and have some breakfast with your sisters?"

Q took a deep breath. His dad would want him to make the best of it, if not for him, then at least for his baby sisters. Akara was nine years old—three years younger than he was—and Amaria was only seven. They were sad and confused, but excited about staying with their favorite Grandma Clara and living near the beach. Of course, they didn't have

to worry about leaving their entire gang of friends behind—or the fact that their grandfather—the Reverend Quincy Washington, Senior, was a stern, quiet and a careful man, not like their fun-loving dad who encouraged Q's daredevil side.

Q grabbed the pillow and returned it to its place on the bed and gathered up the torn pieces of poster and threw them in the trash. He studied himself in the mirror. He looked a lot like his dad—he had the same high forehead, the same piercing brown eyes. *And the same stubborn brain*, he could hear his dad say.

Q shut the door to his room and crept downstairs. He had only lived in his grandparents' house for a week and he still wasn't sure about everyone's morning routine. Back in Brooklyn, he'd help his little sisters get ready while his dad made breakfast, and they'd walk the girls to their school. Then Q and his dad would walk to the bus stop together.

It was during those walks that his father would give him what he called "History Lessons." Sometimes it was about their family and sometimes it was about their neighborhood in

Brooklyn and sometimes it was about contributions African-Americans made to history. Thinking about it now, he realized his dad was teaching him how to be his own man, and how every person, no matter who they were, what they came from, or what their skin color was, could do something with their lives. Of course, back then, he thought those conversations were "BOR-RING!" and "like school."

School! Q hadn't even thought about school yet, since it was June and school was a few months off. There would be new teachers, new friends, and new hallways to navigate. He hated to admit it, but school would have actually been an easier way to find people to hang out with. He decided that his plan for the day would be to check out the neighborhood. His dad always told him that great people didn't wait for things to happen. They made stuff happen! So that's what Q was going to do!

The one thing that Long Beach had over Brooklyn was that the neighborhood that his grandparents lived in was perfect for cruising around on his bike. There were designated bike paths, not much car traffic, and a park across the street to practice his jumps and wheelies. Q grabbed a carton of orange juice out of the refrigerator and made a mental note to check the air in his tires before he set out today.

"Your eyes aren't bigger than your stomach; they're bigger than the glass."

His grandfather's voice snapped Q out of his daydream just as he noticed that his glass was overflowing with orange juice. It spilled from the countertop onto the white polished tile floors.

"Sorry," Q muttered. He turned to grab a dishtowel that normally hung off the stove, except that it wasn't there - because he wasn't home in Brooklyn. He scanned the counters. "I don't know where you—"

"Here." His grandfather handed him a dishcloth. "We keep ours in the second drawer to the left," he said gently.

"Thanks," Q said, wiping up the mess he'd made. He hated these little reminders that he wasn't at home, and made a mental note: *dishtowels, second drawer to the left.*

"Quincy, it's going to take some time," his grandfather said kindly.

"I'm cool," Q insisted. "But call me Q."

"Good morning Q, dear." Q's Grandma Clara joined them in the kitchen and smiled. It was the sort of smile, as Amaria liked to say, "made you forget there was anything bad in the world." Grandma Clara was a short, stout woman who smelled like the flowers that sat in the big plastic buckets next to the fruit stand that he and his dad liked to shop at. *Lilies of the Valley*, Q remembered they were called. At the time he thought it was kind of girly. Okay, it still was kind of girly. But they reminded him of his grandma, so that was okay.

Reverend Quincy Washington was the polar opposite of his grandmother: tall and lanky, with the sort of look that made you want to confess to stuff that you didn't even do! Even though he was stern and held everyone to the same high standards, Reverend Washington was also fair and forgiving. It made him a great choice to be pastor of the local church. But it sometimes made Q nervous, too.

"I'm heading out to take the girls shopping," Grandma

Clara said.

Akara nodded, her mouth full of cereal. "We're getting swimsuits!"

Amaria rolled her eyes. "You need to need to eat your food, not show it to us!"

Akara opened her mouth, revealing a mush of cereal on her tongue.

"Gross!" shrieked Amaria.

Q laughed. His baby sisters could be annoying, but they could also be non-stop entertainment.

"Would you like to join us?" his grandmother continued. "No way!" Q blurted out before he could catch himself.

"I mean, no thanks."

"Are you sure?" she asked, concerned.

His grandfather broke out laughing. "Clara, he's a 12- year old boy, he doesn't want to go shopping with his grandma and his baby sisters."

"I think I'm gonna check out the neighborhood today, any-way," Q told her.

"Okay, we'll be home by supper," she promised. She kissed

Q on the cheek and flashed another Grandma Clara smile and was off.

"Thanks," Q said to his grandfather.

"No problem," his grandfather assured him. "Shopping sounds a little bit like a punishment, and I'm pretty sure you haven't done anything wrong. Yet."

Q laughed. He forgot that his grandfather could have a twisted sense of humor. It made sense. After all, his dad was incredibly funny. He had to get it from somewhere!

"You want to watch some weather channel with me? Looks like rain showers in Wyoming!" his grandfather continued.

Okay, maybe it didn't run in the family. "Uh, no thanks."

Reverend Washington peered at Q over the tops of his wire-rimmed glasses. "Everything okay, Q?"

Q shrugged. "Fine, I guess." His dad used to joke that his grandfather had special powers. *He can read minds!* He'd insist. Maybe his dad was onto something!

His grandfather grabbed the remote and switched off the television. "I know that the last couple of weeks have been difficult. They have for me, too."

Q sat down on the worn brown corduroy sofa that was covered with the quilts that his grandmother liked to make. Sometimes she'd give them as gifts; sometimes she'd donate them to the Red Cross and homeless shelters. His grandparents were always thinking about other people, Q thought. It had never occurred to Q that while he lost his dad, his grandfather had lost a son.

"Your dad would be so proud of you, Q, being so strong for your baby sisters. And I'm proud of you, too," his grandfather said.

Q nodded, not knowing what to say. He appreciated the fact that his grandfather didn't talk down to him like he was a little kid. He got a lot of that at his dad's funeral, people talking to his grandfather and not to him, or patting his head like he was some sort of baby.

"You've had to do more growing up than most people have to do at twelve," Reverend Washington told him, filling up the silence. "I know that I'm no substitute for your dad..." his voice cracked as he trailed off.

Q handed his grandfather his orange juice. He smiled at Q and took a sip, clearing his throat. "All I'm saying is that I know you're a young man dealing with a lot, and if you need to talk to me, I'm here." He set the glass down on a coaster on the oak coffee table and peered at Q.

Q took a deep breath. "It's just that on top of everything else, I have to find a whole new crew to hang out with. For the first time, I kinda miss school 'cause then at least I'd be meeting kids in my grade."

Q's grandfather nodded. "Well, lucky for you there's a place close by where all the local kids hang out—the Real Street Neighborhood Center."

Q shot his grandfather a skeptical look. A neighborhood

youth center sounded kind of lame. But his grandfather was trying.

"Is it close?" Q asked. While he was cool with the fact that his grandfather was having a man-to-man talk with him, there would be nothing worse than being dropped off like he was some little kid.

His grandfather nodded. 'You can ride your bike there. It's on Real Street." He handed Q a post-it note that had directions written out in his grandfather's spidery handwriting and a cobbled together map on back.

Q laughed. "How long have you been waiting to drop this on me?"

His grandfather chuckled. "I was just waiting for you to tell me you're ready. And it sounds like you're ready."

And it's not like Q had anything better to do. "Cool. I'll check it out."

"That's the spirit," his grandfather said as he settled into his burgundy recliner that sat in front of their large-screen television. "Just make sure to be home by dinner."

"No problem!" Q called back. He retrieved his bike from the garage, checked the air in the tires and headed outside. As he stood in the driveway, shielding his eyes from the bright, California sun he realized that he had the entire day to himself. It could be lame but it could also be real cool. The choice was his; he could chase whatever path he wanted. And he was going to chase some action!

CHAPTER TWO

Q BIKED THROUGH the neighborhood, marveling at how quiet the streets of Long Beach were compared to Brooklyn. The streets were wide and smooth, with no potholes or giant cracks in the pavement. Houses were small but well cared for and separated from the sidewalk by perfectly manicured green lawns.

In his new neighborhood everyone had a front yard and a back yard. He passed by the occasional person tending their lawn or washing their car, but unlike Brooklyn, no one was hanging out on their stoop, checking out the neighborhood action. In fact, there wasn't any action in this part of Long Beach, except for the occasional seagull that swooped down into the park across the street. It was a reminder that they weren't far from the beach. Maybe if the Real Street Neighborhood Center ended up being a bust – which he was pretty sure it would be—he could swing by the beach.

He remembered the first time his dad had taken him and his little sisters out here. It was five or six years ago, right after their mom had died. They had practically lived in their mom's hospital room those last few weeks, and his dad wanted to bring them somewhere that was "the exact opposite." So Long Beach it was.

They spent the summer playing in the waves and making huge, elaborate sand castles, only to knock them down again at the day's end. Nights were spent laughing around the dinner table with their grandparents while they finished up the last of their ice cream. Q always begged to stay up just five minutes more so he could hear his father's booming laugh, a sound so loud and deep that his grandfather used to compare it to an earthquake. A sound that he was never going to hear again—

Q saw a boy jamming along the sidewalk just in the nick of time—well, for the boy at least. In order to avoid running him down, Q had to bail from his bike at the last minute. As Q dove into the bushes, the bike careened down the sidewalk until it hit a tree and stopped.

The boy whipped around, pulling a set of ear buds out of his ears. "Whoa! That was insane! You alright?"

Q brushed himself off—a couple of scrapes, but he'd seen worse— and got up. "Why don't you look where you're going, man?"

The boy shrugged nervously. "Um, I don't know. I mean, I was on the sidewalk, y'know?" The boy's hands darted this way and that way as he spoke, like dueling hummingbirds. "Pedestrian right-of-way and all that?"

"Pedestrian-right-of-way and all that?" Q mocked. His venture into the neighborhood wasn't exactly getting off to a hot start. He jogged down the street to grab his bike. It seemed to be no worse for wear. "A sorry would be nice."

"Sorry?" The boy said.

"You're making that sound like a question and not an apology," Q retorted. The boy flinched, and Q realized that he was afraid. "Why don't you try that again?" Q said in a much kinder tone.

"Sorry," the boy said softly.

"Better." Q smiled and then noticed the music blasting out of his headphones. "What's up with that?"

The boy nervously shrugged again and handed Q an ear bud. Q held it up to his ear. Q listened as the beat wove in and out of the melody, seemingly getting lost but then returning again. It was a set of bass tracks overlapping each other in order to form almost a wall of sound. "Hey, that's hot," jamming to the rhythm. "Who is it?"

The boy visibly relaxed for the first time since their run-in. "Me."

"You?" Q scoffed.

"No, really, it's me," the boy insisted, gaining confidence. "Y'see, when you hook up your computer to multiple tracks, you then stagger them so it forms this staccato like ba- ba-da-ba-ba-ba-ba." He sang out the beat. "Then you just start layering them and—"

"Okay, okay, I believe you." Q laughed. Maybe this kid was alright after all. "So music man, what's your name?"

"Oh! It's Jason. Jason Chin. But everyone calls me

Lucky." His hand shot out.

"Good thing I didn't run you over," Q laughed, "or you'd be looking for a new nickname!"

"What?" he looked confused.

"Because then you wouldn't be so Lucky?" Q said, raising an eyebrow.

"Oh, yeah right." *Great one,* Lucky thought to himself. *Now he thinks you're an idiot!* "I thought you were going to punch me out or something," Lucky continued, then winced. Could he sound any dumber?

"Not my style," Q insisted. "The name's Quincy, but call me Q."

"Q. Awesome." Lucky studied Q more carefully. He didn't look familiar. "I've never seen you around here before. Are you new?"

"I just moved here," Q said quickly. "So why do they call you Lucky? Do you win a lot of stuff?"

Lucky could tell that there was more to Q's story when he changed the subject so quickly. He was good at reading people. It's what happened when you didn't have a ton of friends. Or, well, any friends. You spent a lot of time trying to observe other people, figuring out what made them tick. While he hadn't figured out Q, he could tell that whatever the rest of the story was, he didn't want to talk about it.

"No, it's just, well, it's just what they call me," Lucky said, I dunno why."

Now it was Lucky's turn to not want to talk about something. He totally knew why people called him Lucky. It was because he lived in a big house with his parents, who ran a successful restaurant. As an only child, Lucky got pretty much anything he ever wanted. His room was filled with computers and MIDIs and video games and TVs. Whatever the cool new gadget was, Lucky had it.

What the other kids didn't understand is that his parents gave him all of those things to make up for the fact that they were never home. Running a successful restaurant was a "twenty-four-seven job" as his dad liked to say. His mom didn't say much except to yell at him to study in Chinese. Even though they had barely any accent, English was his parents' second language. Lucky grew up bilingual which meant he spoke both English and Chinese, but he sometimes felt that was just another thing that made him different than the other kids. And no matter how much his teachers told him that he was unique and gifted and all those things, the other kids just basically thought he was a freak which is why he lost himself in music.

Of course, he wasn't about to tell his new friend Q that! Chances are he'd find out soon enough. Lucky had only just met Q, but you could tell that he was going to be one of the cool kids at school. He just gave off this vibe like he had it all figured out. So Lucky was just going to enjoy hanging out with him while it lasted. Q would find out that he was the biggest nerd in school soon enough!

"Yo! Earth to Lucky!" Q waved a hand in front of Lucky's face. "So my grandfather told me about this place, the Real Street Neighborhood Center. You know it?"

"Yeah," Lucky replied. He knew about the Real Street Neighborhood Center, or the RSNC as the kids called it. He had checked it out once, during spring break last year. When a group of kids asked him why he wasn't on some fancy vacation with his parents and slumming at the RSNC, he laughed along with them and then snuck back home.

"I thought I might check it out. Whattdya say? You wanna roll with me?"

"Um, yeah, I don't know," Lucky told him. "I'm sorta busy."

Q regarded his new friend skeptically. "Really? 'Cause when I ran into you it looked like you were just jamming in the street. C'mon, it'll be cool. You can hook me up with all your friends. I bet bein' the Music Man, you have hook up around here."

He hopped on his bike and took off down the street, waving for Lucky to follow him. "Let's roll!'

Lucky trotted after Q. *Yeah, all my friends*, he thought.

Awesome.

CHAPTER THREE

The Real Street Neighborhood Center's building and grounds took up nearly half a city block. A tall fence, which was adorned with paper flowers and banners that announced "Pottery Camp" and "Co-Ed Soccer" surrounded it. The building's cinderblock walls were covered in bright graffiti art and murals of the Long Beach community.

As Q and Lucky made their way in through the gate, they had to weave their way through a crowd of six-year-olds dressed in smocks who were gathered in the front yard. Each child stood by an easel and held a paintbrush. A teenage girl addressed the group. "Paint what you see!" she exclaimed, twirling around. The kids attacked the canvas.

Q looked at Lucky. "So is it just a bunch of little kids? Is there any action inside?"

Lucky shrugged. "Maybe in back?" "What's in back?" Q wanted to know.

"Soccer fields, a basketball court, a skate park. That kinda stuff," Lucky replied.

"Now that's the kind of stuff I'm talking about!" Q said. "Why didn't you say that before? I don't just rock the bike; I got a few board tricks, too."

There was a skate park back in Brooklyn, but he had to ride four subway stops to get there. Since his dad wouldn't let him ride the subway alone, he only made it out there every other month or so. He'd get one turn around the ramp before his little sisters would complain about being bored. Maybe the RSNC wasn't so lame after all!

"What are we waiting around here for?" Q exclaimed. "Lead the way!"

"Careful, there's nothing more dangerous than a second-grader with a paintbrush," Lucky warned him as they snaked through the crowd. Q had to jump out of the way to avoid a glob of yellow paint that was destined to become a little boy's sun. They made their way up the steps and through the maze-like hallways, which were covered in photos and artwork.

"Some cool designs out here," Q said, checking out some of the artwork.

"You an artist?" asked Lucky.

Q shrugged. "Y'know, a little bit of this and a little bit of that. A buddy of mine back in Brooklyn, we were putting to-gether a clothing company, we were gonna design t-shirts and stuff! We had some classic designs, but that was before my—" Q stopped.

Lucky waited. "Before your…?"

Q shook his head. "Before I moved. Anyway, this place is killer," Q said. "What's the story?"

There he goes, changing the subject again, Lucky thought. "It's been here for a couple of years," he explained. "Parents wanted somewhere for the kids to hang out in the neighborhood.

They've got all sorts of different programs—music, dance, art..."

"And a skate park. You didn't make that part up, right?" Q asked. He didn't wait for Lucky to answer. "Man, you must be here every second of every day when you're not in school."

Now it was Lucky's chance to change the subject. "Hang on; I'm just trying to remember how to get back there..." The brightly painted hallways were like a maze, but finally Lucky spotted a set of double doors at the end of a hallway that had sunlight streaking through the windows. "Here we go." Lucky pushed open the doors and suddenly they were in back of the building in the sunlight.

Q couldn't believe his eyes. There were kids everywhere! Teenagers were playing a game of pick-up on the basketball court, a bunch of girls were practicing their swing on the baseball field, little kids were squealing as they made their way down the shiny slide, and finally, as Lucky promised, Q saw a small skate park!

They didn't have anything like this in Brooklyn! He made a mental note to come back with his skateboard next time and jogged toward the fenced-off area, momentarily forgetting that Lucky was next to him.

Lucky trotted after him. "Hey, Q! Wait up!"

At the entrance to the park sat a small kiosk that had a sign that read "PAD SHACK" with helmets and pads and other safety gear. A sign read "ALL RIDERS MUST WEAR PROTECTIVE EQUIPMENT." There was also a small crowd of kids who weren't skating. Q made his way to the front of the crowd where he saw two boys facing off against each other. It had all the makings of a fight!

"What? You're too chicken for a rematch?" sneered the larger of the two boys.

This dark haired boy had the air of one of those kids who "knew it all." While the boy was wearing cutoffs and a t-shirt, Q could tell that they were made to look worn in, but were actually pretty expensive. Everyone turned to the other boy with anticipation.

"I don't have anything to prove to you," the other boy spat back. He had blonde hair that was slightly long and fell in his face when he shook his head. "You just can't handle the fact that I'm a better skater than you. I won fair and square, Junior."

"You won, but I wouldn't call it fair and square," Junior yelled back.

Lucky made his way through the crowd and stood next to Q. "That's Junior and Chase. They used to be best friends—"

"Until one of them won…" Q trailed off, keeping one eye on the former friends. The air was electric and it looked like it was going to come to blows. His dad always reminded him that you never needed violence to solve anything. Of course, that was always after Q had gotten in a fight. For right now the guys were keeping it to just words, but it looked like that could change any minute!

"The Long Beach Skate Competition. They hold it every year. Junior, that's the bigger one with the dark hair. His name's really John, but everyone calls him Junior. He won three years running, but last year Chase beat him."

"So Junior can't handle it, and wants a rematch," Q replied.

"Right. He's convinced Chase cheated. But to be honest, Junior's kind of a hothead." Lucky soon realized that everyone had gone silent because they were staring at him.

Junior muscled his way over to Lucky. "You got something to say, Lucky?" The way he said it made it sound like Lucky's luck was about to run out!

"Um," Lucky said, his voice wavering. He looked like he wanted to disappear into the pavement!

"Hey, hey," Q said, inserting himself between Lucky and Junior. "Man, ya'll need to chill out—"

Chase whipped around. "Or maybe you can just mind your own business!" Chase didn't know who this new kid was, but if he was hanging out with Lucky, the biggest nerd in school, chances are he was probably a nerd himself!

Junior stomped back to Chase, getting in his face. "All

I'm saying is that cheating isn't winning."

Chase looked like he was going to explode. He couldn't believe that he used to be friends with this kid! "What did you say?"

Everyone was so silent you could hear a pin drop! Junior narrowed his eyes and took a step toward Chase.

"Cheater."

"Enough!" The voice rang out in the courtyard. Everyone froze. Q spun around to see a man part the crowd and stand between Chase and Junior. "That's enough now," he said more gently.

"He's in charge?" Q whispered to Lucky.

"Yeah, that's Mr. King," Lucky whispered back. "He runs the RSNC."

Q studied the man. He was tall, with a deep, booming voice and kind eyes. There was something about him that reminded him a little bit of his dad. Maybe it was that vibe of calm among the chaos outside. Or maybe it was because he was breaking up a fight! Q had gotten into a few scrapes when he lived in Brooklyn, although the kids he fought with always ended up being his friends.

The fight between Chase and Junior didn't look like it was going to end the same way. "Chase started it," Junior muttered.

"You're a liar!" Chase yelled back.

"I don't care who started it," Mr. King told them, "I'm going to end it. Now." Mr. King looked from Chase to Junior and shook his head. He knew that the second he turned his back, they'd be at it again. He hated to see the two former best friends argue, but he also believed that kids should have the responsibility to choose their own friendships. If they didn't want to be friends anymore, that was up to them. But he was not okay with the situation escalating to physical violence.

"How are we going to fix this?" Mr. King asked them. "I say rematch," Junior said.

"I'm all for it, but we can't rematch here," Chase said, waving toward the skate park. It was the first time Q got a good look at the park. It was small, and there wasn't a halfpipe. The few ramps that were there had been well worn, with deep tracks in the wood. Q understood why wearing pads was a must!

"Well boys, the Long Beach Skate Competition isn't until the Fall. Can you hold off until then? Mr. King looked from Chase to Junior, knowing all too well that he was asking the impossible.

Q stepped forward. " I've got an idea."

All eyes were on him, but Q didn't mind. Being in the spotlight meant people listened to you. It was how you made things happen! And this way all the kids in town would get to see what Q was all about!

"I don't believe we've met," said Mr. King.

"I'm Quincy, Quincy Washington. But everyone calls me Q. I just moved here from Brooklyn. That's in New

23

York." He stuck out his hand and shook Mr. King's hand. His dad always told him a firm handshake was the first step to getting people to listen to what you had to say. It showed that you meant business!

"Hello Quincy, Quincy Washington—I mean Q from New York," Mr. King said, grinning. From anyone else it would have sounded like he was poking fun, but Q realized he was cracking the joke to ease the tension on the playground. Mr. King had remembered someone at church talking about the Reverend Washington's grandchildren coming to live with him. "So what's this idea of yours?"

Everyone waited. Q looked around, taking in the moment. "A rematch," he finally said. "Here at the RSNC."

Junior snorted. "No way. Won't work."

"Junior's right," Chase said. *Yeah, the new kid was a dork like Lucky.* "The park's not in shape for a competition. Sorry Mr. King," he added quickly.

"No worries," Mr. King replied. The boys might not be agreeing, but anything to get them to talk instead of fight was a good thing!

But Q wouldn't let the idea go. "What if we made some improvement to the skate park? An upgrade? Trick it out with some new ramps, maybe a half-pipe...?" He looked from Junior to Chase.

Junior sneered at him, but Chase looked thoughtful. Okay, this new kid Q might be a dork, but he was starting to make some sense. It would be nice to have a half pipe to practice on, even if he had to share it with Junior.

"Sweet, I can totally dig that," Chase said.

Mr. King smiled. "Well, you boys are in luck. Before I was rudely interrupted by your shouting match, I was actually working on a proposal to have the city's maintenance crew do some work on the center. Promise me that you'll hold off on World War Three and I'll let you guys add some skate park upgrades to the plans. Deal?"

Chase's eyes grew wide. "Deal!"

Mr. King turned to Junior, who relented. "Fine. Deal. Whatever." Junior dropped his board on the ground and sped off. A group of boys trailed after him.

Mr. King turned to Q and Lucky. "Lucky, good to see you. Perhaps you and Q and Chase would like to work together, coming up with some ideas for the new park?"

Mr. King felt bad for Lucky. While the other kids were jealous of Lucky's lifestyle, what they didn't realize is that it was pretty lonely. While he had plenty of "stuff," he didn't get to see his parents a lot because they were always working. All of the gadgets in the world couldn't ask you how your day was.

"I don't know," Lucky replied, looking from Chase to Q. He didn't really skate. He was sure once Q found that out, he'd ditch him. At least it made for an interesting day, and he had an unfinished track waiting for him back home.

"Are you crazy?" Q said. "Of course you're going to help!"

Mr. King smiled. Q definitely took after his grandfather. "I've got to get back to work, but I'll be in my office when you're ready to discuss specific plans for the park," Mr. King told them. He headed back into the building, leaving Q, Chase and Lucky all staring at each other.

Q stuck out his hand. "We haven't met. I'm Q. And I know you're Chase, and I'm sure you know my new friend Lucky."

Chase stared at Q's hand like it was something alien. After the whole scene with Mr. King, Chase was ready to reevaluate Q's nerd status. He actually seemed cool, almost confident—like an adult. Except that didn't he know that Lucky was the nerdiest kid in class?

Wait, he's new, Chase thought. Chase waved at Lucky and nodded for Q to talk to him around the corner from the Pad Shack.

"What's up?" Q asked.

"Listen, dude, you seem cool," Chase said. "Which is why I'm telling you that you probably shouldn't be hanging with Lucky?"

Q looked confused. "Whattdya mean? The kid seems cool." He wasn't sure where Chase was going with this.

"He's kind of, well, he's kind of a nerd," Chase said. "So?" Q asked.

"Well, it's just…" Chase trailed off. Q laughed. "Is it catching?"

Chase thought about this for a second. "What? No. I just—"

"Oh, so you think people are going to think I am some nerd too, is that what you're saying?" Q asked.

Finally, he gets it! Chase thought. "Exactly!"

Q looked annoyed. "For real? That's how you're gonna be?"

Now it was Chase's turn to be confused. "What?" "Man, have you ever talked to Lucky?" Q wanted to know.

Chase thought about this for a second. Had he ever talked to Lucky? Except for "you're standing in front of my locker" and "do you know the answer to number eleven?" he hadn't really ever spoken to him. "Well, no."

Q started to get angry. "So what you're saying is that you let the other kids tell you what to think."

Chase snorted. "No, dude, I think for myself."

Q shook his head. "No, you don't. Because you're letting everyone else tell you Lucky's a nerd. You've never talked to him, so you don't know." Chase looked like he was going to say something, but Q was on a roll. "And even if he is a nerd, who cares? He's rolling with me now, and I think he's cool. If you have a problem with it, then peace."

Chase felt his face grow red. He wanted to be angry at Q, except that everything that Q was saying made total sense. He started to feel like a total jerk. "I guess—"

"I guess you've been acting like your former best friend Junior over there," Q said, indicating Junior, who was harassing some of the younger kids.

"Yeah, I guess so," Chase admitted. Ever since he beat Junior at the Long Beach Skate Competition, not only had the two boys no longer remained friends but most of their friends sided with Junior. They believed that Chase had cheated, which wasn't the case at all. He had just been practicing like crazy, while Junior assumed that he was going to win like he always did.

"So what's up? You wanna roll with us and hook up the plans for the most tricked out Skate Park on the West Coast?" Q asked.

Chase nodded. "Sure. And maybe I'll school you guys in a trick or two. Free of charge."

Q laughed. "Thanks, professor." He held out his fist for Chase to dap, and the two boys walked back to where Lucky stood.

Lucky watched the duo approach him from around the corner. This was the part where Chase and Q became best friends and Q told Lucky that he had better things to do. Lucky fished his iPod out of his pocket and started to put in his ear buds when he realized that Q and Chase were standing right in front of him. Waiting.

"Dude, are you gonna stand there or are you gonna help us with the skate park plans?" Q asked.

Lucky looked from Q to Chase and back to Q again. "I'm sorry?"

Chase nodded toward Lucky's iPod. "I think we can grab some speakers from inside and hook that up so we can all listen. My man Q tells me you lay down some insane beats."

Lucky nodded. This was shaping up to be a pretty awesome summer!

CHAPTER FOUR

The alarm went off, blaring mariachi music. Two seconds into the trumpet's plaintive wail, a hand shot out from under the blankets. Instead of shutting the alarm off, it knocked the clock radio to the floor and under the bed, making it sound like there was a mariachi band surrounding him! Los rubbed his eyes and yawned. He always had a hard time waking up, especially since he had a tendency to stay up late. Last night was no different, as he worked late into the evening on his newest project, making one of his bikes more aerodynamic. Los wanted to be an inventor, so he was always working on something new.

The plan was to have his own patent before he got out of high school and a full ride scholarship to MIT. That is, if he could make it out of his bedroom. The room looked like a bomb went off as it was always littered with tools, machine parts, sheets of paper and post-it notes that contained his latest brainstorm. Los insisted that he had an elaborate filing system and that he knew where everything was, but that wasn't totally true—he just said that to get his parents off his back about cleaning his room!

Los fished the clock radio out from under the bed and turned it off, silencing the mariachi band until tomorrow.

After being late to school for three days in a row, his father sat him down to have a talk. His father worked as a designer at Toyota, so he understood that you had to work when inspiration hit. But if Carlos (his dad always called him by his full name when he was being serious) wasn't going to be able to handle his school responsibilities, then his inventing career was going to have to be put on hold.

"It's not that I oversleep," Los explained to him, "it's that

I don't hear my alarm."

Mr. Rodriguez thought about this for a minute and then smiled. "So make your alarm a sound that you really hate. Something that will force you to get out of bed to make it stop. What sound drives you crazy?"

"Easy," said Los, "mariachi music!" He clapped his hands over his mouth as soon as he said it. His parents loved mariachi music, but it reminded Los of too many family gatherings where it was too loud and too crowded and he just wanted to get back to his room so he could work!

His dad broke into a smile. "There's nothing that says we all have to like the same things," he told Los. He left and returned with one of his favorite CDs. "If this will get you out of bed in time for school, then I'm happy."

For the rest of the school year, Los wasn't late once. Thankfully, it was summer now, which meant he could spend the entire day—and night, if he wanted to—working on his inventions. He scanned the room looking for his set of wrenches. He was going to need those later if he wanted to— His baby sister Julissa burst into the room, interrupting

32

his train of thought. "LOS! LOS! LOS!" she screamed in her high-pitched wail.

She was "seven going on seventeen," as his mom liked to say. Julissa took a ton of dance lessons, and his mom was always driving her from practice to recital and back again.

She leapt over the tools and pirouetted onto Los' bed. "LOS!" She said, finally curtsying his way.

She was also a total pain! "Vamanos, Juli!" Los yelled. He was convinced she was going to break something—or hurt herself stumbling over the bike parts that scattered across the floor. Los had been working on his aerodynamics project in the garage, but at night it got creepy, so he had brought everything upstairs. The room was even more cramped than usual.

His sister looked up at him. "It's Julissa," she said seriously.

Los worked to keep a straight face. His little sister fancied herself quite the actress, and she could be very dramatic.

"Julissa," he repeated.

"You'd better come downstairs, Los ugly, if you want breakfast!" she giggled, leaping out of the room with a flourish.

Los shook his head. Julissa could be a typical bratty little sister, but sometimes it was pretty funny.

Los changed into his work clothes—a ratty t-shirt that read "Toyota" – his father was a senior engineer at the plant in town—and a pair of torn jeans. His mom hated the fact that he looked like a mess, but he was always smearing grease and making holes in his clothes while he worked. After replacing a fourth pair of jeans, his mother relented and let him keep a small stash of work clothes that he could get as dirty as he liked!

"Los, that you?" he heard his dad say.

Los walked into the kitchen to discover the entire family at the kitchen table. It was weird seeing them all in the morning on a weekday, since everyone was always rushing off to go to work or school. His older brother Alex flashed him a peace sign while he wolfed down a piece of toast.

His mom drank the last of her coffee and then grabbed his little sister's hand. "We're off to look at dance costumes for Julissa's summer recital." She blew everyone a kiss and they were gone.

Los' dad started to clear away the breakfast plates. "So what're you up to today?"

"I'm still working on the bike project, but since you're here, maybe you can help me out with my plans," he told him.

Los used to run all of his ideas past his dad, but now that he was twelve, he found himself relying more on trial and error, only going to his dad when he was really stumped about something. The great thing about his father is that he never took over, like some dads did. Of course, he wouldn't just give Los the answer, either. This was frustrating when Los had been working on a problem that he just couldn't figure out the solution to, but his dad said that it would help him with critical thinking. He was right, of course, and it felt good to realize that he was the one that figured it out rather than having some-one do it for him.

"Oh, Alex and I figured you'd be working all day, so we were going to check out the car show," his father said.

Alex didn't like to build things like Los did, but he liked to see the end result. He and his dad were both into cars so they took in a lot of local car shows. While Los appreciated the work that went into the shiny, tricked-out machines, he was more interested in what was going on inside than what they looked like on the outside.

"Yeah," Alex said, checking his watch, "and we've gotta mo-tor. We're late."

Mr. Rodriguez smiled at his middle son. "When I get home, I'll check on your progress. But make sure to go out and have some fun, too." And with that, they pushed away from the table and left.

The house was quiet once again. Los sat at the table and thought about his bike that lay in pieces upstairs and was sud-denly hit with the urge to do something else. This was a problem of his—he'd get halfway through a project and get bored. He couldn't help it! There was so much out there in the world, just waiting to be discovered! His science teacher, Mrs. Booker, discussed his "lack of follow through" with his parents but Los was lucky enough to have a father who understood that there was just so much that he wanted to do, to see, to create, that the possibilities could be overwhelming. His dad would laugh in that way that he did and tell him that that was the point of being in seventh grade: the possibilities were endless!

Los put his dirty breakfast plates in the dishwasher and decided that possibilities were the name of the game for the day. Maybe he'd see what his friend Chase was up to. Chances are he was hanging out at the RSNC. There was always something new to work on there!

CHAPTER FIVE

Los hopped on his back-up bike—he had three or four bikes at any given time, each like a Frankenstein monster assembled out of various parts—and made his way over to the Real Street Neighborhood Center. It was only a mile or so from his house, and his parents had actually moved to the area because of the great neighborhood program they had for kids.

However, a couple of summers ago his dad had been laid off and together they discovered that the RSNC wasn't just for kids. Mr. King invited Mr. Rodriguez to tag along with Los and Alex, and the second their dad walked in the door, he was hooked! There was always a building improvement project to work on, or classes on carpentry or design to teach.

While he knew it was a financial strain on the family, Los thought it was great having his dad around - even if he had to share him with Alex. His mom picked up the slack, teaching a full class load that summer, as she was a Professor of History at the University of Long Beach. Now that his dad was back at work she only taught a couple of classes so she could watch Julissa during the day. She would joke that she needed some girl time to compete with all the men in the house.

Although to be honest, between his mom and Julissa and his dad and Alex, Los found himself with a lot of time alone.

But sometimes he preferred it that way—it's how he got everything done, after all. He realized that he should be happy. His parents didn't treat him like a little kid, they weren't breathing down his neck and checking up on him all of the time. But he had to admit, it did sometimes get a little lonely.

Thankfully he had his best friend Chase and the RSNC. He realized that Chase had probably been at the Center all morning, trying out some new moves on the three or four skate ramps that they charitably called the skate park in the back of the building. He started to pedal faster, enjoying the breeze that blew from the water. That was the other nice thing about their neighborhood. Not only did they have the RSNC, but no matter how hot it got during the summer, the ocean always kept everything cool.

Los pulled up to the front gates of the RSNC, which was buzzed with activity. The younger kids were playing Red Rover and there were a few boys and girls practicing for the upcoming dance recital – the same one that his mom and Julissa were shopping for. His mom made the entire family come to all of Julissa's various performances– there were the singing lessons and the dance recitals and the kids' theatre. But to be fair, his mom made sure that Julissa came to the Science Olympics and to the ceremony when he won "Best Young Designer" in the Toyota Car Design contest. Although that stuff was interesting! Not like some stupid jumping around in a tutu!

The kids all waved and yelled after him as he walked in the front door. Everyone knew Los because Los was the one that could cure a sticky wheel on a skateboard or fix the broken arm of a doll. He had his dad's "magic touch" as his mom liked to call it. If it was broken, he'd figure out how to make it better. He hadn't figured out how to fix the problem of sharing his parents with his older brother and younger sister, but he figured he hadn't really applied himself to the problem yet!

He waved and smiled as everyone yelled "Los!" It was a nickname he picked up when his dad volunteered at the center that one summer. Since his dad was Carlos Senior and he was Carlos Junior, there had to be a way to tell them apart. There was no way that Los was going to go by "Junior" like John Charger Jr. did. He didn't want to be confused with the biggest bully at Long Beach Middle School. Everyone said that Junior definitely took after his dad, John Charger Sr., although Los hadn't really had any run-ins with Junior's dad. He was on the City Council, so it's not exactly like they were hanging out!

Los spotted Chase working with an African-American kid he didn't recognize and Lucky. It was weird seeing Lucky at the RSNC since he never hung out there. Chase had always said that Lucky probably thought he was too good for the place, but Los always suspected that Lucky was shy. He didn't talk a lot and always wore his headphone, jamming along to some unheard beat.

"Yo! Chase!" Los bounded over to the three boys and hit

Chase up with a high-five. "What'cha workin' on?"

Q, Chase and Lucky were bent over a big sheet of paper, working on what looked like a drawing.

"It's the design for the new skate park," Q said, then bent back down over their work. "The half-pipe goes here, at the edge, because you gotta build the bleachers for an audience.

Then here you have the—"

Los sized up the plans in about ten seconds. He didn't know who this Q kid was, but he did know that he had everything backwards! "That's the wrong place for the half-pipe—"

Chase was about to introduce Q to his best friend when

Q fixed Los with a look. "And you are—"

"Los. Los Rodriguez." Los Shook Q's outstretched hand. "Hey, Lucky." He nodded at Lucky, who shrugged offered the faintest hint of a smile. "Good to see you around."

Lucky smiled. "Hey." His summer was really looking up, although for the past hour he, Q and Chase and been scratching their heads trying to figure out how to put the new skate park together. After Mr. King had given them the goahead to come up with a building plan, it soon dawned on them that now they'd actually have to do it. The result of their work was a sheet of paper with a few squiggles and a lot of eraser marks.

"Los is kinda a design genius. He can build anything," Chase told Q.

Q raised an eyebrow. "Really? Did you build that sorry-looking bike that you walked back here with?"

"You mean the one with the solar-powered fan, the aerodynamic handlebars that fold in half for easy storage?" Los countered.

Chase and Lucky shared a look. It looked like Q broke up the fight between Chase and Junior only to start one with Los!

The air was tense while Q and Los sized each other up.

Finally, Q broke out into a wide grin. "Man, why didn't you say so? Okay, we are lost with a capital L, so now that Los is here, unloose us, willya?"

Q slid over to let Los in. Lucky and Chase exhaled. They were back in business!

"Here's the problem," Los said. He pointed out that they needed to switch the ramps and the half-pipe so there was adequate space for "takeoff and landing" for each of the riders. "You don't just finish a trick and automatically come to a stop. There's some drag," Los explained. He grabbed the pencil from the table, flipped the sheet over, and started drawing.

"You guys need help?" a female voice asked. The boys looked up to see a studious-looking girl with her hair in a ponytail.

Los waved at her. "Nope, Jazz, I got it," Los said. "But if you want to come check out—"

"This is guy stuff," Q interrupted, "you wouldn't be interested."

Jazz raised an eyebrow. "Guy stuff? Really."

Los bit his lip, trying not to laugh. Jasmine King was Mr. King's daughter and a total force of nature! She was unpredictable and sometimes slightly crazy – kind of like her nickname, Jazz. But Q was going to have to learn that lesson for himself!

"Um, Q, this is—" Chase jumped in, trying to salvage the moment.

Q wasn't having any of it. "We're tricking out the skate park, per Mr. King's instructions," he told Jazz, as if daring her to say more.

Jazz smirked. "First of all, Mr., King is my dad, and second, making a few changes to the skate park is hardly guy stuff."

Q rolled his eyes. "Oh, you skate?" Q knew some female skaters back in Brooklyn, but they were usually the girls who hung around the guys they had a crush on. They weren't serious skaters.

Jazz turned to Chase and pointed to his skateboard. "May I?"

"Be my guest," he said, handing her the board and his helmet.

Jazz strapped the helmet on and dropped the board onto the nearest ramp. Cresting up the side, she executed a perfect kickflip to rail grind. Then she skated back to Q.

"Thanks Chase," she said, handing Chase his skateboard and helmet. "See you guys around!" Jazz waved and left.

Q watched her leave in amazement. "Man, I've never seen anything like that."

Lucky chuckled. "You've never seen anything like

Jazz."

That Jazz was something, Q thought. What that something was, though, he wasn't quite sure!

"Let's finish up these plans and get them to Mr. King so we can get this skate park happening!" Chase declared. The boys huddled around the project, working to make their vision a reality.

CHAPTER SIX

"Rise and shine!" Chase's mom, Julia, pushed open the curtains to his room, letting the sunlight stream in through the window. Like a supersonic laser it hit Chase right in the eyes, blinding him.

"A little less shine, mom" Chase complained as he rolled over. His mom was what was known as a "morning person." She was always full of platitudes like "the early bird gets the worm" and "early to bed, early to rise." He loved his mother, but when he was tired, he wished she was a little less...cheery.

"It's time to get up!" she said again, a little less cheery. Chase rolled over and put a pillow on his head. He only had two times of day: time to skate and time to eat. Everything else was simply waiting for skating and eating!

"You said you wanted to be up early today, Chase," his mom reminded him sternly.

It suddenly hit him. "The skate park! Right!" He scrambled out of bed. He was pretty sure that his friends might make fun of him if they knew that instead of an alarm clock, his mom woke him up every day. But since she and his dad split up, he didn't get to see his dad much, if at all. It was nice to have the reminder that there was at least one parent around who cared that he was there!

"I'll be down in a sec, mom."

"Okay, Chase," she said, smiling. She closed his bedroom door gently.

They were breaking ground on the new skate park at the RSNC today! Mr. King was impressed with the plans they had come up with – well, the plans he, Lucky and Q talked about; Los had really done all of the actual work. Mr. King had scanned the plans and emailed them to the contractor, who said the whole construction process should only take a few days! Mr. King praised them all for their dedication to the project, but Chase really knew that it was all directed at Los.

Chase was sometimes slightly jealous of the fact that Los was so inventive, and that Mr. Rodriguez clearly took pride in his son's accomplishments. The last time he had seen his dad, Mr. Anderson wanted to know when Chase was going to give up skating and "concentrate on his studies." Like he was going to give up skating! It was the one thing he felt like he was truly gifted at, like the one thing he was born to do! Unlike school.

Chase always hated school. Teachers always blamed it on his parents' divorce, but they had separated when he was two and divorced when he was three so he never remembered it any other way. No, he had problems concentrating in school. It was like they would start to talk about fractions and then suddenly his mind would be going a mile a minute about this and that and suddenly thirty minutes had gone by and he had missed the entire lesson! It wasn't until last year when he had been diagnosed by his doctor with ADD and working with a therapist on different tricks and tips to keep his mind focused that his grades started pulling themselves out of the gutter.

But it had also taken a lot of work – a lot of hard work, and that took away from his skate time. His mom didn't want him to give up skating, but she did want him to do better in school. She asked him what the one thing she could do to help his skating, and he said keep the in-ground swimming pool in the backyard empty. So his mom made him a deal – apply himself during the school year, get his grades up to passing, and he could have an empty pool to skate and practice in all summer. He got his grades up, and his mom kept her part of the bargain. He was probably the only kid in Long Beach who was excited to have a place not to go swimming in!

Chase dug under the piles of clothes that littered his room, looking for his favorite pair of skate pants and a longsleeved t-shirt. Even though it was hot out, even with proper safety gear, it was easy to get road rash from falling down in the pool, so he liked to keep covered. He ran downstairs to find his mom finishing up breakfast at the kitchen table.

"So this rematch sounds like a pretty big deal," his mom said, concerned.

"Which is why I've got to practice," Chase replied.

The night before that he realized the whole reason revamping the skate park came up was because of his upcoming rematch with Junior. And since the skate park was going to be out of commission, he needed to practice!

Mrs. Anderson wasn't a huge fan of skateboarding, because

she worried that he might get hurt. However, she appreciated fact his dedication and all of the effort he put into it.

"I've got to get to work, but make sure you wear your helmet, okay?" She kissed the top of his head.

Chase sighed. "I always wear my helmet!" He might have ADD, but he wasn't crazy!

His mom laughed. "I know, I know, but I'm a mom, it's my job to worry."

"Hey mom, d'you think dad would come out to the competition?" Chase asked. He normally saw his dad every other weekend and a couple of weeks during the summer, but his father hadn't been able to come out to see him win the Long Beach Skateboard Competition. It had been one of Chase's proudest moments, and he wanted his dad to see that he was a success.

"You know your dad travels a lot for work during the summer," his mom said kindly.

Chase sighed. His dad didn't just travel for work a lot during the summer; he traveled a lot for work period. He had missed his last two weekends, and they hadn't nailed down plans for when Chase would stay with him over summer vacation. The rematch with Junior wasn't just about having a second chance to prove that he was the best, but it was a second chance for his dad to come out and watch him tear it up!

Chase's mom kissed the top of his head. "Tell you what. You let me know when it's going to happen and I'll work on him. Now how about I get some hamburgers to grill for dinner?"

"Sounds good, mom," Chase said, trying not to sound disappointed.

He knew that it wasn't her fault. She was just trying to prevent him from being disappointed. But since he wasn't a stellar student, skateboarding was his way of showing everyone that he was good at something, and he wanted to show his dad that too.

Whether his dad made it to the rematch or not, one thing remained the same: he had to practice if he wanted to win.

Chase grabbed his skateboard and took the stairs two at a time. He had already beat Junior once, and he hadn't cheated. He was going to beat Junior again, just to prove he was the best!

CHAPTER SEVEN

By the time Chase showed up, Q and Lucky were already there, talking to Mr. King and the contractor. Q noticed Chase and motioned for him to join their group.

"Cool, am I right?" Q asked.

Chase couldn't believe that it was all really happening. Two days ago, he and Junior were having a throw-down on who was the best, and today a new skate park would be built for them to prove it.

The construction crew was taking down the fencing that surrounded the Real Street Neighborhood Center's existing skate park to let the backhoe through. Lucky and Q were looking over the construction plans with Mr. King.

"Can I see the finished plans?" Chase asked.

Lucky moved aside to let Chase through. "You can see how we have the half-pipe set up, with the stands here," Mr. King pointed out. "You boys did a great job."

Chase was impressed. It looked like a state of the art skate park!

"Dude, this so rules. I can't believe we get to skate this!"

Chase high-fived Lucky and Q. He pointed out one of the jumps. "I can't wait 'til I'm flying over that!"

As Chase and Q discussed the awesome tricks they'd be able to rock out on the new half-pipe, Lucky studied his new friends. It was weird to say that: friends. Lucky had always been pretty shy. It was true that his parents gave him a lot, but that's because they were making up for the fact that they were never at home. They owned one of Long Beach's most successful Chinese restaurants, and it was, as his dad liked to say, a "twenty-four-seven job."

His parents had hoped that Lucky would take over the business, but when he was seven he was diagnosed with bad allergies. His dad didn't think it was sanitary for him to be working with food when he had a perpetually runny nose, so Lucky got to stay home instead. That's when he started getting into music. He appreciates the fact that they weren't pushing him into the family business, but a DJ with the sniffles wasn't exactly cool!

"Isn't that right, Lucky?" Q looked at him expectantly. "What?" Lucky had been so lost in thought that he hadn't heard what Q had said.

"The booth is gonna be killer, right?"

"Oh yeah, killer!" When Los was finishing up the plans the previous day, he included a small DJ booth so they could do a "spin and skate." Lucky didn't even know Los knew he was into music! For the first time in his life, he felt like he was living up to his nickname – in a good way.

"Guys! Hey, sorry!" Los rolled up, looking like he had slept in his clothes.

Q studied him for a moment. Maybe Los had slept in his clothes. "Man, weren't you wearing that yesterday?"

Los looked down at his outfit and shrugged. "Um, no? Yes? Maybe? I don't know. I don't really pay attention."

Chase held his nose and waved at the air. "P. U. Dude, you totally wore those clothes yesterday."

"Hey, I'm like Einstein. The guy had one outfit!" Los insisted.

"Actually, Los, he had multiple outfits," Lucky informed him, "but they all looked exactly the same so he didn't have to worry about what to wear. He wore the same thing every day."

Los sighed. "Okay, so I'm no Einstein. I'm working on it!" They all cracked up.

Mr. King interrupted them. "Guys, come over here," Mr. King called after them, "I want you to meet Jack Taylor, he's the contractor from the city." Mr. King nodded toward a heavy-set man with a bushy white beard and glasses – Q thought he sort of looked like Santa, if Santa worked construction when he wasn't delivering presents. "Jack, these are the Real Street Kids."

"The Real Street Kids, that's pretty cool," Q mused. He stuck out his hand. "Quincy Washington, but you can call me Q. These are my boys Chase, Los and Lucky." The boys all shook hands with Mr. Taylor.

"So which one of you boys is our budding architect?" Mr. Taylor wanted to know.

Los raised his hand shyly. "That's me, although I prefer to think of myself as more of an inventor."

Mr. Taylor laughed, which sounded like a big, angry seal. "Anyone who builds anything is a little bit of an inventor, aren't they? Well, Los, your plans were great. We just had to make a few minor tweaks to get them to adhere to the Long Beach City Codes and we were good to go. If you're looking for an internship when you hit high school, you make sure to look me up!"

Los smiled. It was one thing to be creating stuff in his bedroom, it was another to see it being built in front of his very eyes! Or about to be built, as the backhoe was slowly creeping into the lot, ready to knock over the existing skate park. This was his favorite part of designing anything – seeing his dreams become reality!

Mr. Taylor pulled out a walkie-talkie. Static crackled through the speakers and he pressed a red button. "We're set to go."

The construction crew sprung to life and the backhoe started with a growl. It inched forward, and Q, Lucky, Los and Chase watched as the huge constructed equipment demolished the ramps in the park, reducing them to rubble in a manner of minutes.

"Awesome!" cheered Los.

"Ooh, that's painful," Chase said, covering his eyes. The skate part at RSNC had been the place he learned to skate. He had been coming there since kindergarten, right after his parents got divorced. The second he saw kids catching air in the skate park, he was hooked. His mom joked that he probably saw more of Mr. King than he did her. While that might not be true, he did see Mr. King more than he saw his own father.

He snuck a glance at the head of the RSNC, who surveyed the scene proudly. Mr. King caught Chase's eye and gave him the thumbs-up. Sure, they were destroying a part of his past, but they were building something for his future – a new and improved skate park was pretty cool. Where he was going to defend his title as the Long Beach Skate Champ!

Los thought it was just as interesting to see things being taken apart as it was figuring out how they were put together. Demolition was another part of construction and design that he didn't get to do a lot, because both of his parents pronounced it "dangerous." But here at the RSNC, had a front row seat! He couldn't wait to see his creation take shape.

Lucky slipped on his headphones so the demolition of the skate park had a soundtrack all its own. The ground shook as the backhoe snapped a ramp in two. He thought it felt like the drum beat to a song. Fishing his cell phone out of his pocket, Lucky set it to record. He could probably work in the demolition sounds on a new beat. In fact, he could debut the track when the skate park re-opened. He grooved to the imagined melody.

Q watched everyone as they were all lost in thought. His dad always said he was good at bringing people together. At the time, Q didn't understand how that was important, or even a good thing. But standing here now at the RSNC, he suddenly

understood exactly what his dad meant. With the right people –
and the right friends – they could accomplish anything. It was
like a little bit of his father had come back that moment. It was
a good feeling…

…which was interrupted by a man yelling. "STOP! STOP
THIS INSTANT!"

Everyone whirled around to see a thin, balding man in a suit
running toward them, waving his arms. He had watery blue
eyes and thin lips that were pulled back into a perpetual sneer.

"You're a little overdressed for the breaking ground ceremony," Q remarked. Chase high-fived him. The man ignored Q
and rushed over to Mr. King and the contractor. He thrust a
piece of paper into their hands and then started motioning to-
wards the skate park and to the RSNC main building and back
to the skate park again.

The contractor said something into his walkie-talkie and the
backhoe slowed to a stop. A crowd of kids turned from the
demolition site to the men, who were clearly arguing. Jazz ap-
proached the boys, looking nervous.

"That's Mr. Charger," she said in a conspiratorial whisper,
"Junior's dad. He's on the City Council." "He looks a little
wound up," said Q.

Lucky pulled out his ear buds. "If he's here, that's not a good
sign. He prevented my parents from redoing their restaurant
a couple of years ago. They had done everything by the rules,
too. My mom said he just likes to hold everything up and
make trouble."

"Can he do that?" Chase asked.

Los looked confused. "The Contractor just said everything was done to code." Los understood that there were rules and regulations that came along with building something. It was to keep everyone safe and make sure that the plans were sound.

"Why would he want to make trouble?" Q asked. "This is a neighborhood center. I mean, I've been here just a couple of days and I can tell that it's a good thing."

"Mr. Charger clearly doesn't think so," said Lucky. He motioned toward where the three men stood. Mr. Charger was shaking his head, clearly saying NO to everything that Mr. King and the Contractor were throwing his way.

"You think Junior has anything to do with this?" Chase asked.

Q spun around and spotted Junior in the crowd. The boy who had been ready to come to blows the day before was looking like he wanted to disappear.

"He looks like he wants the ground to swallow him whole, so I'd go with a no," Q said. "Although maybe it's just from having a dad who's all-around embarrassing. So glad my dad's not like that. Or wasn't..." Q trailed off and snuck a look to see if anyone noticed. It's not that he wanted to keep the fact that his dad wasn't around anymore from his new friends. He just didn't want anyone feeling sorry for him or treating him special.

Thankfully, his crew was all still fixated on John Charger, Senior, who was shaking his head with one final NO. He turned and addressed the crowd.

"Everyone, everyone gather around!" He motioned everyone to step closer. "Your Mr. King has made a mistake. The City Council only approved interior improvements to the Real Street Neighborhood Center. He never got the authorization to make improvements to the skate park or any of the outer areas. So we're going to have to shut this down."

Q stepped forward. "Okay, so we get approval and construction can continue. Nothing to worry about, people."

The city councilman looked at Q like he was something he found at the bottom of his shoe. "And who might you be?" "Quincy Washington," Q said, giving Mr. Charger his

full name. Only his friends called him Q, and this guy might be on the Long Beach City Council, but he certainly wasn't his friend. Or anyone's, for that matter!

"Well, Mr. Washington," Mr. Charger said in his most patronizing tone, "construction will continue only IF the council approves the plans. And from what I've seen of the plans, that doesn't seem likely."

Los looked crestfallen. The plans were his! Maybe this was all his fault?

Lucky tapped him on the shoulder, as if reading his mind. "Not your fault, Los. Remember, Mr. King got the Contractor, people checked it out. Nothing to do with you." Mr. Charger looked sideways at Los.

"Maybe if the plans weren't created by...a twelve year

old…at any rate, we're done here. Good day."

Mr. Charger turned to leave, but Chase yelled after him. "But Mr. Charger! Mr. Charger!" Chase waved his hand at the City Councilman to get his attention. "What are we going to do for a skate park? It's totally thrashed!"

He pointed to the rubble.

Mr. Charger smiled, but it made him look more evil, if that was even possible! "I guess you should have thought of that before you started."

Chase spun around to face Junior. "Do something!"

Mr. Charger snorted. It was as close to a laugh as he could probably muster, thought Q. "This is adult business. Taxpayer business. This is not the business of children. Perhaps you'd all do well to remember that."

At this, Junior slammed down his skateboard and took off back into the RSNC's main building. For once, Chase actually felt sorry for Junior. Maybe Chase's dad wasn't around a lot, but when he was, he wasn't a jerk!

Mr. Charger turned back to Mr. King. "Oh, and for your gross negligence, I'm afraid that your contract with the city and the Real Street Neighborhood Center is hereby terminated."

A hush fell over the crowd. Mr. King was the RSNC! Q, Lucky, Los and Chase watched helplessly. They couldn't believe it had come to this!

"Wait, you can't do that!" Jazz yelled after Mr. Charger. "That's not fair!"

"Life's not fair, Miss King. If anyone has a problem with it, they can bring it up with the City Council. Good day."

Q, Chase, Lucky and Los looked at each other with a mixture of shock and horror. They had begun the day, excited that they were going to demolish the old skate park and build a new one. But the only thing they had accomplished was demolishing Mr. King's career.

And for the first time since they had all become friends, the Real Street Kidz were speechless.

CHAPTER EIGHT

"I can't believe it," Los lamented, his head in his hands. "This is all my fault."

The boys sat at one of the picnic tables surrounding the former skate park. A gentle breeze blew in off the water, kicking up dust and debris from the abandoned construction.

Lucky coughed and waved his hands, trying to clear the air. "Actually, it was Q's idea."

"So you're saying it's my fault?" Q asked, jumping up. "How was I supposed to know he needed special permits and stuff? I'm just a kid!"

"Well, you should have known it shouldn't be that easy!" Chase yelled back, getting in Q's face. "Everything was great until you showed up!"

"Yeah, you were going great, about to get flattened by Junior!" Q retorted. Now Q and Chase were in each other's face. They stared each other down.

Lucky realized that this was about to get real bad, real fast. He got between them.

"Guys! GUYS!" The normally quiet Lucky put his arms out, separating them. "The only person's fault it is Mr. Charger's! I bet he didn't even have to fire Mr. King. He just did because he's a jerk."

Q breathed heavy, still buzzing from the adrenaline from the morning's events. His grandfather would probably give him a lecture on calling grown-ups jerks, but Lucky was right. And in the case of Mr. Charger, the Reverend Washington would probably even agree!

Los nodded. "You know, he's always trying to get in the way of improvements around here. A couple of years ago, he wanted to tear the place down."

That was the year his dad was out of work. Mr. Rodriguez supervised the construction project that brought the building up to code. Working on the building brought his dad in contact with a bunch of new people, and one of the moms who was doing fundraising for the project was a hiring manager at Toyota. If it hadn't been for his tenure at the RSNC, his dad might not have found a new job. Except now it was Mr. King who was out of work, and without it, it was looking like no one would have the RSNC to escape to!

Chase shook his head. "Sorry, dude." He held out his fist to Q, who tapped it with his own.

"Don't worry about it, man," Q responded.

"So what now?" Lucky asked. He had just made this new group of friends at the RSNC. It would be just his luck to have it all taken away!

"Yeah, without Mr. King there's really no RSNC," Los worried out loud.

"Which is why," Q interjected, "we figure out a way to get him his job back."

"You think?" said a voice behind them. The boys whirled around to see Jazz standing there, arms crossed. She didn't look happy, but no one did after the scene that had just taken place!

"We've got a plan," said Q, a touch defensively. He didn't dare say it out loud but he did feel kind of responsible

for Mr. King getting fired. If he hadn't suggested the new skate park, this morning would have never happened!

"Your first plan got him fired," said Jazz matter-offactly. "Let's hear it."

"Well, we're coming up with one is what I mean!" Q said. "Yeah, that's what I thought," said Jazz as she stalked off. "Yikes," Lucky said as they watched her go.

Los shrugged. "Take it from me, it's tough when your dad is out of work. She's just worried, is all."

"But she doesn't need to be, because Q is coming up with a plan!" Chase said confidently. "Aren't you, Q?"

Q scowled, and turned away from the group. He started to pace, wearing a path into the dusty ground.

Chase, Los and Lucky shared a look. They had only known Q a couple of days but he always seemed to have it together. He seemed to be at a total loss.

Q was feeling the same way. *Think, think!* It's like his brain had given up in protest. Q stopped suddenly and turned to face the group.

"I have an idea," he said. "We're going to stage a protest," Q told his friends.

Chase, Los and Lucky looked at each other, confused. Chase finally spoke. "How do you do that?" he asked.

He had seen protests on TV, but he wasn't exactly sure how they got there.

"It's kind of a lot of work," Los said uncertainly.

"No, no, it'll be a snap!" Q promised. "But we gotta act, like now."

Lucky leapt up. "What do you need?"

"That's what I'm talkin' about!" Q said. "Okay, huddle up." Lucky, Chase and Los gathered around him, forming a circle. "Lucky, since you're our Music Man, I'm gonna need you for the sound system."

"Got it," said Lucky, He couldn't believe that a couple of days ago, he was just jamming along the street solo, and now he had his very own band of friends.

"Cool. Now Los, I'm gonna need a stage," Q said, turning to Los.

"That's kind of a tall order," Los said. "When do we need this all done by?"

"No, no, it'll be a total breeze, I promise!" Q said. "Let's say tomorrow, two o' clock. Right here at the RSNC."

"What should I do?" Chase asked.

"Glad you asked," Q replied, "you're going to be in charge of signs!"

"Signs?"

Q nodded. "Yeah, maybe round up some of the kids who were in art class? That'll look good on camera."

"On camera?" Lucky wondered.

"Yeah, that's my job," Q told them, "I'm gonna get the media here to cover the whole thing. It's gonna be huge, right?"

"Right!" yelled Lucky and Chase.

Q looked at Los. "We need you to be a part of this." "You really think we can have this together by 2 p.m. tomorrow?" Los asked.

"We have to," Q replied. He put his hand in the middle, and Chase and Lucky covered it with their own. They all looked at Los.

"You in?" asked Q.

Los relented. "Yeah, I'm in. Of course I'm in!" He put his hand on top.

"Real Street Kidz on three," Q instructed them. "One, two, three!"

"REAL STREET KIDZ!" they yelled.

CHAPTER NINE

Q let himself in the house with his key. It was weird to have just one key to open the door, even though it worked on a lock and the deadbolt. Back in Brooklyn, he had two keys that his father gave him on a chain that he could attach to the belt loop on his jeans. He still wore the chain, but the keys were gone. Q imagined that the new tenants of the apartment he shared with his father and his sisters had them now. He wondered if Mrs. Bendetto brought them marinara sauce every Sunday night like she did for his family? She'd always say she "cooked for an army," but Q suspected that Mrs. B. knew his dad was a terrible cook!

"Quincy, is that you?" he heard his grandfather call out. "Yeah, it's me," he replied, shutting the door. Was his grandfather ever going to catch on that he wanted to be called Q?

"I didn't expect you back so soon," Reverend Washington said. "You want some lunch?"

"I'm good," Q said. He walked over to the refrigerator and poured himself some orange juice.

"So how'd the ground breaking go?" his grandfather asked.

"Not exactly as planned," Q said, "we kinda got Mr. King fired."

His grandfather turned off the TV. "Fired?"

Now Q had his full attention! "It turns out that there's some city guy who really has it out for Mr. King. He said that there weren't permits or something. But don't worry I have a plan." He rinsed out his glass and put it in the dishwasher and turned to go upstairs.

"Hang on a second Quincy," his grandfather said. He pointed at the sofa. "Why don't you sit down and explain to me exactly what happened, and what exactly your plan is."

Q sighed. "I don't see what the big deal is."

"The big deal is that I need to know what's going on in your life," his grandfather said sternly.

"Maybe you need to understand that I have it all under control!" Q shot back.

"Quincy—" his grandfather began – "I mean Q, all I'm saying is that I'd like to know what's going on in your life. Your grandmother and I don't know you very well. Not because we don't want to, but with the distance between Brooklyn and Long Beach, well, we just didn't get out as often as we wanted to."

The distance between Brooklyn and Long Beach was something Q had thought about a lot in the past couple of days. While he was meeting new friends and finding his way around his new hometown, he felt like the more comfortable he was here, the harder it was to remember what life had been like when his dad was still alive. And that was something he didn't want to forget.

"This wasn't how I wanted to bring the family closer together," his grandfather continued. "If I could change it, I would. I don't want to replace your dad, Q."

Q nodded but said nothing.

His grandfather smiled. "You have to understand that I was a father before I was your grandfather. That just doesn't go away. You may look at me and think I'm old and gray but I've gathered a little bit of wisdom and understanding along the way."

"I'm not a little kid," Q told him.

"Then let's discuss like adults," his grandfather replied. Q couldn't come up with an argument for that. He sat down across from his grandfather and told him the entire story: Q's idea for the skate park, the plans, Councilman Charger barging in, Mr. King getting fired. He ended the story with his new friends and their plans for a protest.

His grandfather listened to the whole story, and when Q was done he leaned back against his chair, his hands forming a steeple in front of him. "A protest. Now that takes me back. What can I help you with?"

"We don't need any help," Q said.

"I'm not saying you need it Q, I'm asking if you would like some. I've organized plenty of protests back in the day."

"I've got this one covered, Gramps," Q assured him. "It's not as easy as you'd think," his grandfather said, concerned.

"Don't sweat it, seriously. Are we good?"

His grandfather nodded. 'The only thing that matters is that you're good, Q."

"I'm great," Q assured him. "Now I've got a protest to plan."

Q spent the evening at the computer, even skipping dinner so he wouldn't lose a single second of time. He emailed news outlets to let them know about the protest, sent his friends reminders of their assignments, and posted on local message boards, inviting the community to join the cause to get Mr. King his job back.

A knock at his bedroom door startled him. He checked the clock. It was nearly 11pm!

"Come in!" he said, stifling a yawn.

It was his grandmother. "Quincy, what are you still doing up?"

"Just finishing up everything for tomorrow," he said, "but I'm going to bed in a couple of minutes. Promise."

His grandmother chuckled, and for a moment Q was reminded of when his mom was still alive, how she'd come tuck him in at night. Of course, he was too old for that now, but he didn't want to hurt his grandmother's feelings.

"That's exactly what your dad used to say," she said, smiling. "And then in the wee hours of the morning I'd hear him rustling around in his room, reading comic books by flashlight. You're old enough to decide when you need to go to bed, just make sure you get plenty of rest for tomorrow." She kissed the top of his head and left, closing the bedroom door gently behind her.

Q yawned and shut down his computer. By this time tomorrow, Mr. King would have his job back thanks to Q and his friends. And everyone would know who he was. Not too bad for his first two weeks in Long Beach!

CHAPTER TEN

Q showed up at the RSNC around noon. The first thing he noticed was the throngs of seven and eight-year olds set up in the front yard of the Center, painting rainbows and suns on poster boards.

"Do you like it?" a little girl in a pink jumper asked. "Sure," said Q, "but what's it for?"

"For the protest!" she said brightly, and then attacked the board with more paint.

The protest? Q thought. He looked around and spotted Chase sitting under one of the large trees that provided some shade in the Center's front yard.

"What do you think?" Chase said proudly, waving to the groups of kids. "I got 'em together, just like you asked."

"I asked you to have them make protest signs," Q said. Chase frowned. "Yeah, they're here, they're going to protest. With signs!"

"No!" Q said. He took a deep breath and collected himself. "Chase, you were supposed to get them to make protest signs. Stuff that talks about our cause! Signs that say things like 'Hire Mr. King' and 'Mr. King is the RSNC.'"

"Well, you didn't say that," Chase said. "I thought you'd know what I meant!"

"How am I supposed to know? I've never done a protest before!" Chase yelled. He couldn't believe it! He did everything just like Q asked and this is how he was thanking him? "I've been here since nine this morning, unlike you."

"I was busy making sure Channel Four – oh, nevermind." Q stalked off in the direction of Los, who was hammering together a framework for the stage.

"Los, man, you've got like, an hour. You're not done with the stage yet?" Q asked.

Los grabbed a rag out of his back pocket and wiped the sweat from his face. "I told you this would take time. It's not like I have anyone helping me."

Q inspected Los' work. "It looks fine, just slap a piece of plywood over it and you're done."

Los shook his head. "It doesn't work like that, Q, I gotta make sure it's safe first. If you don't build the foundation correctly-"

"No one's gonna see the foundation and I'm the only one that's going to be on stage," Q instructed him, "so just nail the top on and you're good to go. Besides, I need your help with the protest signs, since Chase kinda messed that one up."

"But Q…" Los trailed off, realizing that Q had already moved on. "Can we protest the protest?" he asked to no one in particular.

"Hey Lucky!" Q called out to Lucky, who had set up his laptop and a couple of speakers on a folding table.

Lucky didn't hear him, because he was wearing ear- phones and jamming away to some unheard tune.

At least one of them got it right, Q thought, waving his hands in front of Lucky's face to get his attention.

Lucky tapped his mouse pad and slid the earphones down around his neck. "I've got some killer tunes," he told Q.

"Tunes?" Q asked, confused, "I was wondering where the megaphone was?"

"A megaphone? Where would I get one of those?" "How else am I gonna be heard over the crowd? You at least brought a microphone, right?" Q asked, irritated.

"You said to bring a sound system," Lucky said nervously, "so I brought my sound system."

"This is it? You brought your DJ equipment? How are people gonna hear me?" Q yelled. He stalked off, not even waiting for Lucky's answer. He strode over to the stage and was intercepted by a woman in a suit who was followed by a cameraman.

"Excuse me, are you..." she fumbled for his name, "Q Washington?"

Q nodded and stuck out his hand. Thankfully something had gone right! "I am, you must be Miss Enderfield?"

The woman smiled. "Call me Claire. We thought we'd get

some establishing shots, then we'll set up over there," she said, pointing toward the front of the stage. "That way we get a front row seat to all of the action. If you don't mind, we'd like to follow you around and ask a few questions."

"Sure," said Q.

Claire led him over to where Chase and Los were trying to convince the seven and eight-year olds to make protest signs. They didn't look like they were winning the battle, as evidenced by the unicorns, rainbows, and heart signs that littered the lawn. Claire led them into the middle of it all and pointed at her cameraman to start shooting.

"I'm Claire Enderfield, here with Q Washington, who has organized a group of kids down at the Real Street Neighborhood Center to…well, Q, why don't you tell us why we're here."

"We're here to protest the firing of Mr. King from the

RSNC," he said.

"So you organized this all by yourself?" Claire asked.

"I did," Q said. "It's a lot of work, but I thought it had to be done."

Los and Chase looked at each other. "By himself?" Chase asked.

"I didn't realize he was here at six a.m. building the stage," Los grumbled.

Lucky ran up to where Los and Chase were standing. "Hey

guys, it's two pm. Should we let Q know?"

"He'd hate for us to interrupt his TV time," Los said. "Hey Q!" Chase yelled, "It's two!"

Q smiled and waved. *Didn't they know he was giving an interview?* "I should get going, but make sure to get right in front so you can catch the whole thing," Q told the reporter. He wove his way through the crowd of parents, kids, and neighbors who wanted to see what all the hubbub was about. He leapt up on the stage and felt it wobble. Steadying himself, he made a mental note that if he just stayed still, everything would be fine.

"Parents, friends, residents of Long Beach, thank you for joining me here today!" he said. No one noticed that he was up on stage! He waved his hands over his head. "Ladies and gentlemen, if I can get your attention!"

He noticed a group of parents go over and admire the artwork of the children who were supposed to be making protest signs. Spotting Los, Chase and Lucky in the crowd, he motioned for them to help. But they just stood there with their arms crossed!

Q saw that the camera in front was rolling. He had to turn this protest around! "Excuse me, if I can get your attention!" No one responded. He jumped up and down, waving his arms like a madman. "EXCUSE ME!" he screamed.

He knew the second he landed that it was the second jump that caused the stage to collapse underneath his feet. Everyone turned just as the entire two-foot structure came tumbling down, with Q on top of the heap.

Claire Enderfield was the first to reach him. "Are you okay?" she asked.

Q brushed himself off and realized the entire crowd had formed around him and the cameras were still rolling! Lucky stuck out a hand to help Q up, but he brushed Lucky off. "I'm fine."

Claire turned back to the camera. "This is Claire Enderfield, live from the stage collapse at the Real Street Neighborhood Center's protest to get Mr. King's job back. Thankfully, no one was injured. But in this reporter's opinion, the complete mess of today's protest highlights the fact that the kids down at the RSNC need a stronger, more disciplined hand than Mr. King, who allows the kids here too much freedom. Hopefully the Long Beach City Council, under the direction of John Charger, will institute someone better qualified to guide the children of Long Beach. This is Claire Enderfield, signing off from the RSNC."

Claire nodded to the camera and then turned back to Q, who stood watching in horror. "Thanks so much for inviting us down here!" she said cheerily as she waved goodbye.

The crowd trickled away, leaving Q, Los, Chase and Lucky huddled around the demolished stage. Q held his head in his hands, not knowing what to do. It was a wish he had wished a thousand times in the past few weeks, but he meant it more than ever.

He wished his dad were here.

CHAPTER ELEVEN

Los, Chase and Lucky looked at each other, not knowing what to do. Q was sitting on the ground with his head in his hands, rocking back and forth. He wasn't saying anything.

"Listen, we were just angry, but it's okay," Los stammered.

Lucky sat down next to him. "People mess up, Q. It happens."

Q shook his head and stared at the ground.

"Hey, we all messed up today," Chase said, sitting down on the other side of Q. "I should have asked you what you meant when you asked me to make signs."

"And I should have told you that making the stage was impossible," Los said. "you could have really gotten hurt."

Q swallowed hard. "I didn't give you a chance," he said quietly.

Los shrugged. "Friends should always be able to be brave enough to say no. Or tell you when you're wrong. So I messed up, too."

"The worst part of this is that it's not that I messed up," Q said, "it's that I messed up getting Mr. King his job back." "No,

I think the worst part is that you messed up," a voice said. Everyone turned to see Jazz standing over them.

She sat down across from Q. "When you see that footage on the evening news, you'll understand what I mean." She started to giggle.

"The look on your face when you realized the stage was gonna give," Chase said, "oh, man." He started to chuckle.

"It was pretty funny," Lucky agreed, laughing.

Q looked at Lucky, Chase, Los and even Jazz laughing at the total disaster he had created. "I guess I can cross protest organizer off the list of things I want to be when I grow up," he finally said.

This made everyone laugh even harder, and suddenly the events of today were turning into a distant memory.

As the laughter died down, Jazz stood up. "Okay, now it's time to get to work."

"Work?" Q asked.

"It's time to figure out a plan that'll actually work," Jazz said. "Unless you can't handle working with a girl."

Q waved her on. "I can handle working with anyone if they've got a good idea. The floor is yours, girl."

Chase leaned over to Los. "What does having the floor have anything to do with it? We're outside."

Los shushed him. "It's just something people say."

Jazz tapped her foot as she waited on Los and Chase. "Any time you guys are ready…"

"Hit us," said Los.

"I think I know someone who can help." Jazz said. "His name is Sam Madison, and he's known my father forever."

"So it's old friends month? I don't get how that helps," Q said skeptically.

Jazz sighed dramatically. "If you'd let me FINISH."

Los and Chase chuckled. They were used to Jazz, as they had known her since they had been coming to the RSNC

for as long as they could remember. They forgot how frustrating she could be if you didn't know her!

Q waved her on. "Go ahead."

She continued. "Sam Madison is the guy who finances all of the non-profits my dad's worked with over the years. He's like, the RSNC's biggest donor."

Chase looked confused. "So he's going to run the place now?"

Lucky shook his head. "No, no, Chase, the guy who has the money!"

Chase thought about this. "So he's going to give us money to build a new RSNC?"

"No, Chase," Los smiled. His best friend could tear it up

on a skateboard like no one's business but sometimes his ADD made it difficult to follow one thought process to the next. "Sam Madison has money. So the City Council will listen to what he has to say."

"Or at least give him a chance to speak up for my father," Jazz added.

"Right, whatever," Los said. That was pure Jazz. She always had to get in the last word!

Q turned to Jazz. "So how do we get a hold of this Mr. Madison?"

"Dad's got the number in his office," she said brightly, and then her face fell. "I mean, in his old office."

Q thought Jazz could be pretty annoying, but he also knew what it was like when the future was uncertain and you didn't know who you could rely on. Knowing that there were friends to get you through the rough stuff helped. Today had been a little bumpy, but it also showed him that his friends were going to stick around. Even when he was being kind of a jerk!

"C'mon," he said to Jazz gently. "We've got a call to make."

Mr. Madison not only took their call but also invited them down to his office to discuss the matter further. Los knew the bus schedule like the back of his hand, having memorized it "for fun" a couple of summers ago. He got them on the right bus, which led them into the heart of downtown Long Beach.

Sam Madison's office was on the 15th floor of a modern

building in Long Beach's business district.   Everything was glass and steel and quiet. Their footsteps echoed on the marble floors as they made their way to Mr. Madison's suite.

"This place would be rad to skate," whispered Chase. His voice echoed down the hallway.

Lucky broke out into a nervous laugh. He didn't know if his parents would approve of him getting so involved. He hoped they would be done by dinner so he could get home before his parents walked in, but he wasn't about to leave his new friends. His parents might not understand that, but he'd find a way to make them get it!

Q studied the large corridor lined with granite and marble. He appreciated the fact that you probably had to make bank to work here, but it seemed kind of cold.   Impersonal. He wasn't sure what he wanted to do when he grew up – but whatever it was, it was going to be filled with people and music and laughter. It wasn't going to be a mausoleum like this place! Suddenly he was nervous. What if Mr. Madison was exactly like this building? Was he going to listen to a group of 12 year olds?

Jazz led the group down the hallway to the last office, which read MADISON INDUSTRIES in huge silver letters on the door. She opened it and waved them inside.

"This place is amazing!" Los marveled. He liked to see how buildings were set up and how the architect had used various elements to create the overall look. Maybe there was a future for him in building design? Sometimes he thought his biggest problem is that he liked to do too many things. Although their biggest problem right now was getting Mr. King his job back!

The receptionist was about to ask them their names when a short, squat man with a bushy mustache and an inviting smile came out to greet them.

"Jasmine! Boys! I'm Sam Madison. C'mon in my office!" He shook everyone's hand enthusiastically.

Q exhaled. This Sam Madison wasn't stuffy or cold at all. His confidence grew as Mr. Madison nodded to the receptionist and led the group through a maze of hallways until they reached a heavy black door that read "Sam Madison, President." He opened it and let everyone in.

"Sit anywhere," Mr. Madison instructed them as he moved a pile of papers from the couch to make room for everyone. He grabbed his desk chair and wheeled it to the middle of the room while everyone got comfortable. Q admired the view out the window. You could see all of Long Beach, from the other office buildings to the neighborhoods to the ocean!

Mr. Madison followed Q's gaze. "Being president of your own company has its perks," he said with a wink. "Like having to play hardball sometimes. Why doesn't someone bring me up to speed."

Q, Los and Jazz filled him in on the events of the past few days, with Chase and Lucky providing occasional commentary. Mr. Madison asked few questions and nodded a lot, writing things down on a lined yellow notepad. When the story had ended, he tapped his pen against his forehead thoughtfully. "Well, there's one thing here that seems to be absolutely clear."

"What's that?" asked Q.

"City Councilman John Charger is kind of a jerk," he said.

The group burst out laughing. Q liked it when adults didn't treat you like you were a baby just because you were young. He might not be an adult yet, but that didn't mean that he didn't have good ideas. He caught Jazz's eye and gave her the thumbs-up. Mr. Madison had the hook-up!

"However," Sam Madison continued, "I can't force the

City Council to do anything they don't want to do." "Why not?" asked Chase.

The businessman laughed. "I like the way you think, son."

"But they can't all be like Mr. Charger, can they?" asked Los.

"Yeah, he's really our big problem," added Lucky.

Mr. Madison shook his head. "No, he's just a special case. You know why he hates your dad, don't you, Jazz?" Now it was Jazz's turn to look confused. "No! Why?" "Because John Charger Senior once had a crush on your mom," he told her.

Jazz looked so horrified that Q couldn't help busting up at the look on her face. It was weird to think of your parents ever dating.

"But everyone's an adult now," Los said, confused.

Mr. Madison shook his head. "Just because someone's an adult doesn't mean that they don't hold a grudge, or have all the answers. There are plenty of adults who don't always act that way. Even your parents. But hopefully everyone does the best they can."

Chase had never thought about his parents that way. He had always assumed that his dad was too busy because he wasn't interested in what Chase was doing, or that Chase wasn't good enough. Maybe his parents were just doing the best they could.

"Anyway Jazz," Mr. Madison continued, "your mom went to Homecoming with your dad and the rest, well, the rest is history."

"Jazz! Junior could have been your brother!" Q teased her.

"Okay, today has been gross enough without that image in my head!" Jazz laughed for the first time since her father had been fired. Everyone in the room relaxed a little bit. Maybe it was going to be okay.

"That aside," Mr. Madison said, "they've been wanting to build condos on the RSNC land. They've offered to open the RSNC in a new area, but that's new construction, new permits. It would be years before it would be ready to re- open."

"So what you're saying is that if we play hardball with them" Q said, "that they may not go for it."

"Yup," Sam Madison said seriously, "that's exactly what

I'm saying."

Jazz looked crestfallen. "So there's nothing we can do?" "I didn't say that, but let me work on it. While the City Council may be interested in the money that a new condo develop-ment would bring in, they also have to be elected by a public— a public that would rally around a neighborhood center. There's a meeting tomorrow."

"So we need to get people to this meeting tomorrow," Q interjected.

"Exactly," Mr. Madison said, pointing at Q. He got up and showed everyone out, promising that he would be in touch before tomorrow night.

Q hung back. "Mr. Madison?" "Yes, Q?"

"Mr. Madison, I kind of feel like this whole thing is my fault, so if there's anything I can do – if there's anything you need, will you let me know?"

Mr. Madison smiled. "Q, I listened to that whole story and I can promise you that you didn't cause this. This ball has been set in motion years before you were even born."

"I know, but—" Q started to say.

Mr. Madison cut him off. "But the fact that you feel responsible means you're just a stand-up kind of guy. I don't see a lot of that these days, so I can promise you this much: if there's something I need, I will be the first to let you know."

He handed Q his business card. "That's how you can get a hold of me if you come up with any bright ideas."

Q slipped the card into his back pocket. "Thanks."

He knew that he had just been paid a huge compliment from a rich and powerful man, but Q still felt about two inches tall.

CHAPTER TWELVE

It was standing room only in the room where the Long Beach City Council met. The Real Street Kidz had kept their promise to fill the room and the place was packed with parents, kids, and the members of the City Council. The buzz in the room was that there was something afoot.

Councilman Charger kept checking his watch, waiting to call the meeting to order. Chase, Los and Lucky waited outside with Jazz, just like Q had told them to. He had called earlier in the day to say that he and Mr. Madison had come up with a plan, which was great!

Except that Q – and Mr. Madison-- were nowhere to be found.

"I hope this isn't some sort of joke," Jazz said, checking her watch. "Because it's not funny if it is."

"They're going to start any second now," Los said worriedly. As someone who constantly slept through his alarm, he understood how easy it was to be late, but this was the most important meeting of their lives!

"Excuse me boys," said a familiar voice. "Dad!" Jazz said hugging her father fiercely.

Mr. King smiled at Los, Chase and Lucky. "I've been told to report to this meeting, but no one's willing to tell me why. I don't imagine any of you have an idea?"

Chase, Lucky and Los all shook their heads no. They were telling the truth! Q hadn't exactly opened up about what the plan was. Now they were beginning to think Jazz might be right and it was all part of some elaborate prank!

"I'd better find a seat," said Mr. King. The boys stepped aside to let him through.

"I'm going in with my dad," said Jazz. "If Q doesn't show up, he'd better make sure he never shows up anywhere in Long Beach ever again!"

For once, Chase agreed with Jazz. He looked from Los to Lucky. "You guys? Anyone hear from our main man? I don't even have a number for him."

Lucky grabbed his cell phone and scrolled through his address book before he realized: "I don't have a number for him either."

Los shrugged. "Me neither."

"I don't even know where he lives," admitted Lucky, "we just ran into each other on the way to the RSNC."

"Yeah, did he say why he even moved here?" asked Los. Chase shook his head. "I just know that he's from

Brooklyn. That's it."

"Maybe he didn't have a plan," said Lucky weakly, "and he was too embarrassed to tell us." Lucky felt like he was betraying Q, his first real friend. But Q had a tendency to play things pretty close. Maybe he felt like he had gotten in too deep and couldn't get out.

"I kinda feel bad," Los admitted.

"Yeah," Chase added. "It's like, maybe we just assumed Q would smooth everything over 'cause that's what he's been doing since he got here. Maybe he didn't feel like he could ask for help?" Chase thought about how he felt before he was diagnosed with ADD, like he was drowning in his studies but he was too embarrassed to ask for a life preserver!

The three of them were silent while they realized they didn't really know anything about their new friend, except that he always seemed to have things figured out.

Just then the sound of footsteps rang out down the hall. It was Q!

"Sorry I'm late!" he cried out, as he ran down the hall- way. An older African-American man with graying hair and glasses followed him. "Guys! This is my grandfather, Reverend Quincy Washington. Gramps, these are the Real Street Kidz, Chase, Los and Lucky."

His grandfather smiled proudly. "You boys are doing something good here today." He looked at Q, and his eyes started to water. "Your dad would have been so proud, Quincy."

They were only words, but Q was knocked flat by how much those words meant to him, coming from his grandfather. He didn't even notice that his grandfather had called him by his full name. Q smiled and nodded, saying nothing, swallowing a lump in his throat. He needed to pull it together. He had a job to do here today!

But for the first time since the car accident, he felt like his dad was with him, cheering him along.

"Okay guys, let's do this." Q straightened his tie – if you wanted to be taken seriously you had to dress seriously – and flung open the door to the Council meeting just as John Charger banged his gavel, calling the meeting to order.

Q and the rest of the gang found a place to stand in back while the room quieted down.

Mr. Charger addressed the crowd. "This meeting will come to order. Our first item of business is discussing improvements to the sewage system—"

"No, it's the Real Street Neighborhood Center!" someone called out.

Mr. Charger shook his head. "I'm sorry, but we have an agenda here—"

"We want to talk about the RSNC!" another voice cried out.

"There is a way that these meetings are run, people, it's called parliamentary procedure—" Mr. Charger said, his voice rising.

The room began to chant. "RSNC! RSNC! RSNC!" The floor shook as they stamped their feet and clapped along to the rhythm of the words. Q watched Mr. King break out into a shy smile, in awe that all of these people had come out to support him!

The difficult part hadn't been getting them out – the second that Los set up his email blast and Lucky, Chase and Q manned the phones, people were willing to do anything to show their support for Mr. King. The word had spread through the neighborhood like wildfire. Now if they could only change the City Council's mind!

John Charger Senior's face flushed red as he banged his gavel, attempting to get the crowd to quiet down. But the louder he banged, the louder they became, soon clapping their hands and stamping their feet. The entire room reverberated with "RSNC! RSNC! RSNC!"

"I don't see the harm in starting with the RSNC, John," said a woman who sat behind a nameplate that read "Councilwoman Ayres."

The room broke out in applause. She smiled and waved, shushing everyone.

"Fine," said Mr. Charger none-too-happily, "we will table the sewage dilemma to discuss the issue of the Real

Street Neighborhood Center."

"Do we have someone speaking on behalf of the Center tonight?" asked Councilwoman Ayres.

Everyone in the room turned around, waiting to see who was going to step up to the podium in front of the room.

Q took a deep breath. "That's me!" he squeaked. He took a deep breath and calmed himself. *You can do this*, he told himself. *You bring people together, just like dad said.*

"That's me," Q said more confidently, striding to the podium. He straightened his tie. All eyes were on him! He took a stack of note cards out of his jacket pocket and addressed the room. "Ladies, Gentleman, and Members of the Long Beach City Council," Q began.

"I'm sorry," John Charger said, cutting him off, "but as you are not a taxpayer or a registered voter, you have no business in having the floor."

"But I'm here on behalf—" Q started to say.

"You are here on behalf of no one," said Mr. Charger, as snidely as he could. "You are a child."

Q looked around the room, panicked. Now what? Everyone was counting on him. He caught his grandfather's eye. Reverend Washington winked – he winked! – and stood up straight, reminding Q that he had every right to be there.

Councilwoman Ayres pleaded with him. "Can't we just hear what the boy has to say?" "According to our rules of order, we don't have to," replied Mr. Charger.

"According to the rules of order, he may speak on behalf of a registered voter or taxpayer. And he does," called a voice from the back of the room.

"And who might that be?" asked Mr. Charger skeptically.

"Me," said the voice.

Everyone turned to see Sam Madison make his way to the podium where Q stood. "This is Quincy Washington. And Quincy Washington speaks for me. Last time I checked, I paid some pretty hefty taxes, but if you'd like me to go home and get my tax return to prove it, Mr. Charger, I'm sure all of these fine taxpayers would be happy to sit patiently."

"Fine," Mr. Charger sighed, "let him speak."

Mr. Madison clapped Q on the back. "Knock 'em dead, kid."

Q took a deep breath and stood up straight. "Members of the City Council, my name is Quincy Washington, and I recently moved to Long Beach with my grandparents after my father was killed in a car crash a month ago."

The room went silent. Chase, Lucky and Los shared a look. They had no idea that Q was dealing with something so heavy. He seemed so together…they couldn't even imagine being in his shoes. If he hadn't already proved that he was pretty awesome, this cemented it.

"I found my way to the Real Street Neighborhood Center, where I met my friends Lucky, Los, and Chase. I didn't need to be in town long to realize that the RSNC is a vital part of the community, for kids and parents alike. Kids need a place to go, and parents need a place where their kids will be challenged and safe. Under the guidance and inspiration of Mr. King, the RSNC provides both."

Jazz looked at Q with a newfound respect. Maybe he did know what he was talking about! And he was kind of cute when he was defending the RSNC!

Q continued. "After Councilman Charger, acting on behalf of the Long Beach City Council fired Mr. King for lacking the necessary permits to make improvements to the RSNC's skate park, my friends and I sought out the owner of the RSNC's building and property, local businessman Sam Madison."

Jazz snorted. Her father looked at her and shook his head. She was the one that had told Q about Mr. Madison! It would be nice to get just a little credit! Maybe Q wasn't so cute after all.

"After meeting with Mr. Madison and telling him about Mr. King's firing, he has instructed me to inform the Long Beach City Council that he's no longer interested in leasing the RSNC building to the City."

A hush fell over the crowd. Lucky's mouth dropped open. Los turned to him.

"Does this mean what I think it means?" he whispered. "I don't know!" Lucky replied.

"I don't get it, what's going on?" Chase asked. Lucky and Los waved him off.

"As the lease on the RSNC is up at the end of June – in less than ten days – the RSNC will be closed until further notice," Q said.

"No way!" Chase blurted out, then clapped his hands over his mouth. No one heard him, because the room was abuzz with the news! The RSNC, shut down? What would they do? Where would they go?

"This was your great plan?" Jazz hissed at Q.

Mr. Charger banged his gavel on the table, bringing the meeting back to order. "Quiet. QUIET!" The roar dissipated into a murmur. "Is that all, Mr. Washington?"

"Not quite, Mr. Charger," Q responded. "Fine," he said with a sigh, "continue."

Q fumbled with the note cards he was using, trying to find his place again. "Mr. Madison has hired private contractors who have gone over the plans with the city, and made all necessary adjustments so that the plans for the new skate park are both safe and up to code."

"So if we approve them, he'll continue to lease the building to us?" Mr. Charger asked hopefully.

"Under one condition," Q said, putting down his note cards. This part he knew by heart.

"Yes?" Councilwoman Ayres.

"The Real Street Neighborhood Center will remain open and all new construction will be funded by Mr. Madison himself… on the condition that Mr. King is reinstated as the head of the RSNC," Q concluded.

The room broke into thunderous applause. He caught Mr. Madison's eye, who gave him the thumbs up. He then saw his grandfather in the corner of the packed room. Reverend Washington pointed to the ceiling, nodded, and smiled. Q knew what that meant. It meant that his dad was watching him, and his dad would be proud.

"Quiet!" Mr. Charger yelled over the din of the crowd. "Mr. Madison, you know that the Long Beach City Council Development Committee, chaired by me, has been looking at the RSNC land to develop it into a condo community. Perhaps your idle threat is exactly what we need to push us toward that resolution?"

The crowd grew silent. Q had rehearsed this part with Mr. Madison, in case it came up. He looked to Mr. Madison, who nodded at him.

Q swallowed the lump in his throat and crooked the microphone neck so the Council wouldn't miss a single word. "Councilman Charger," Q said solemnly, "do you really want to be demolishing a popular neighborhood youth center during an election year?"

Cries of "hear hear!" and "you go Q!" and "Mr. King! Mr. King!" reverberated off the walls. Mr. Charger banged his gavel, trying to get control of the meeting again, but it was too late. People were stamping their feet and clapping their hands, chanting "Mi-ster King! Mi-ster King!"

Q looked around at the chaos and smiled. He confidently turned back to the council members. "I would now ask that you call for a vote to reinstate Mr. King."

The crowd grew silent as they watched the vote go down the line. Out of the five council members, they needed a majority, or three ayes.

"Aye," said the first.

"Aye," said Councilwoman Ayres, who smiled at Q.

The vote was to Mr. Charger. He had no love for Mr. King, but Q could see his comment about an "election year" had shaken him up.

He cleared his throat and squawked out "aye."

The applause was so loud that they didn't even hear it read into the official record that Mr. King had his job back. They didn't need to. Everyone crowded around Q and Mr. King, congratulating them.

Mr. King turned to Q. "So I have you to thank for this?" he said with a smile.

"It's not just me, I was just the mouthpiece." Lucky, Chase and Q squirmed through the crowd to greet Q. "I couldn't have done it without these guys."

"Your friends," Mr. King said. Yeah," Q smiled. "My friends."

Life was going to be different in Long Beach, living with his grandparents. And just when he got over the death of his mom, his dad was taken from him, too. But Q realized looking at Los, Lucky and Chase that he was going to be tight with these guys forever. Together, there wasn't anything they couldn't do.

99

And that was pretty cool.

"Real Street Kidz in the house!" Q yelled, pumping his fist in the air.

"Real Street Kidz!" Los, Chase and Lucky called back.

EPILOGUE

Two short weeks later, the RSNC cut the ribbon on the new and improved skate park. It looked amazing! There were multiple sets of ramps for skaters of all ages, a half-pipe with a small audience viewing area, and a DJ booth where Lucky was busy spinning records.

The crowd was humming with anticipation, as today was the long-awaited rematch between Chase and John Charger Junior.

A beat shook the ramp and Lucky tore things up from the DJ booth. "Step right up for the Inaugural run on the Real Street Neighborhood Center Skate Park! A rematch of the Long Beach Skate Competition between Chase Anderson and John Charger Junior!"

Lucky's voice echoed through the park as the gathered crowd began to applaud.

"Ready?" said Junior.

"I've been ready for weeks," Chase said.

"Yeah, we thought you needed the extra practice time, that's why you sicced your dad on the place," said Q.

"Dude, I had nothing to do with that. I have been itching to wipe the floor with your friend here."

Chase shook his head. "I don't need to smack talk." "Because you're afraid?" Junior taunted him.

"No," said Chase, "Because I'm that good."

He nodded to the judges and trotted over to the half-pipe for his first run. It was especially bright today. As he balanced on the lip of the half-pipe, he noticed someone in the crowd frantically waving at him. Chase shielded his eyes and focused on the waving person. It was his dad! He gave him a thumbs-up and his dad gave him a thumbs-up back.

Chase took a deep breath and dropped into the half-pipe. No matter what happened today, he had already won.